JAN KARON

PRESENTS

✦ CYNTHIA COPPERSMITH'S ✦

Violet Goes to the Country

story by MELANIE CECKA

pictures by EMILY ARNOLD McCULLY

VIKING

For Kyle, Alicia, Ryan, and Brandon. —M.C.

Viking
Published by Penguin Group
Penguin Young Readers Group, 345 Hudson Street, New York, New York 10014, U.S.A.
Penguin Group (Canada), 90 Eglinton Avenue East, Suite 700, Toronto, Ontario, Canada M4P 2Y3
(a division of Pearson Penguin Canada Inc.)
Penguin Books Ltd, 80 Strand, London WC2R oRL, England
Penguin Ireland, 25 St Stephen's Green, Dublin 2, Ireland (a division of Penguin Books Ltd)
Penguin Group (Australia), 250 Camberwell Road, Camberwell, Victoria 3124, Australia
(a division of Pearson Australia Group Pty Ltd)
Penguin Books India Pvt Ltd, 11 Community Centre,
Panchsheel Park, New Delhi – 110 017, India
Penguin Group (NZ), 67 Apollo Drive, Mairangi Bay, Auckland 1311,
New Zealand (a division of Pearson New Zealand Ltd)
Penguin Books (South Africa) (Pty) Ltd, 24 Sturdee Avenue, Rosebank,
Johannesburg 2196, South Africa

Penguin Books Ltd, Registered Offices: 80 Strand, London WC2R oRL, England

First published in 2007 by Viking, a division of Penguin Young Readers Group

1   3   5   7   9   10   8   6   4   2

LIBRARY OF CONGRESS CATALOGING-IN-PUBLICATION DATA
Cecka, Melanie.
Jan Karon presents Cynthia Coppersmith's Violet goes to the country / story by Melanie Cecka ;
pictures by Emily Arnold McCully. — 1st ed.
p. cm.
Summary: During a trip to the country, curiosity and excitement get Violet, the little white cat, into all kinds of trouble,
much to the dismay of Alice's uncle, who "was never much of a cat person."
ISBN 978-0-670-06181-5 (hardcover)
[1. Cats—Fiction. 2. Country life—Fiction. 3. Curiosity—Fiction.] I. Karon, Jan, date- II. McCully, Emily Arnold, ill. III. Title.
IV. Title: Cynthia Coppersmith's Violet goes to the country. V. Title: Violet goes to the country.
PZ7.C29993Jag 2007
[E]—dc22
2006038979

Set in Kennerly
Manufactured in China

Love covers all transgressions.
—Proverbs 10:12

𝒱iolet was a little white cat with bright green eyes. She lived in a bookstore with a lady named Alice, and people always said the two of them went together like milk and cookies.

In the mornings, Violet helped Alice wash the breakfast dishes or water the flowers in her garden. When the shop opened, Violet was there to greet the customers, and to give her opinion whenever it was needed (and sometimes when it wasn't). But the evenings were Violet's favorite time of day. That's when Alice took Violet onto her lap and brushed her fur until it gleamed. "From nose to tail, from ear to ear," Alice always said, and Violet knew without a doubt that she was loved.

One evening after brushing Violet's fur, Alice began to fold her clothing into a suitcase.

"We're going to the country," Alice said, "where my aunt and uncle have a little farm. Just think: milking cows, picking apples, gazing at the stars. Won't it be heavenly?"

Violet had seen pictures of barns and cows and apple orchards in books. But this would be her first trip to the country, and she was as curious as could be.

The next morning, Alice bundled Violet into a picnic basket, and they set out. Towns and buildings gradually gave way to rolling fields, and in no time at all, they had arrived at a small farmhouse that sparkled with a fresh coat of yellow paint.

Aunt Lydia was as short and boisterous as Alice was tall and gentle. They hugged and laughed and hugged again. Uncle Leo didn't say much.

"This must be your dear cat," said Aunt Lydia, reaching down to pet Violet. Violet rubbed her back against Aunt Lydia's legs to say hello. She turned to greet Uncle Leo, but he was already headed upstairs with Alice's suitcase. "Never was much of a cat person," he said over his shoulder.

Aunt Lydia chuckled. "Oh, don't mind him."

As Alice and Aunt Lydia chatted, Violet pushed the screen door open with her nose and slipped out onto the porch. There was a tidy, red barn, a fenced paddock where sheep grazed under a spreading oak, and a kitchen garden with ginger-colored pumpkins and winter squash peeking from among the vines. Behind the barn lay the fields, now fallow for the season, and rows of fruit trees, their leaves already touched with the golden hues of autumn.

Violet could hardly contain her excitement. It was everything she had imagined! Should she climb up to the hayloft and choose a spot for a nap? Or perhaps she would head for the pasture and see if sheep were really as wooly as they looked in picture books. Yes! That's what she'd do.

As Violet trotted across the yard, she turned to see a line of downy chicks trailing a hen like railcars behind a steam engine. *Real chickens*, thought Violet. This was far better than any book!

When the mother hen went *peck, peck, peck*, the chicks went *peck, peck, peck—peep!* When the mother hen fluffed her wings, the chicks went *fluff, fluff, fluff—peep!*

What were they pecking at? Violet crept closer to get a good look. But the mother hen had spotted her. "Get back!" she warned Violet. "Back! Back! Back!" She darted at Violet in a great flurry of feathers and squawks. "Back! Back! Back—*peep!*" the little chicks twittered. And back Violet skittered . . . right into Uncle Leo's path.

Now, Uncle Leo had been heading to the barn with a stack of paint cans. He hopped right, then left, then right again to avoid stepping on Violet. And the tower of cans swayed left, then right, then left again until finally they tumbled to the ground with a *whump! whump! whump! whump!* Paint splashed the gravel like yellow rays of sunshine.

The hen and chicks squawked and scattered.

Violet could see Aunt Lydia and Alice leaning over the railing to get a better look. "Are you all right, Leo?" called Aunt Lydia.

"I'm all right, but I can't say the same for the paint," Uncle Leo replied. "I was going to use it for the henhouse, but the hens will just have to make do with what they've got. Thanks to this blasted cat. . . ."

At that, Violet took off for a space beneath the porch steps, leaving a trail of yellow paw prints behind her. She stayed there for the rest of the afternoon, coming out only when Alice coaxed her with a dish of milk.

"What a fine mess!" Alice said when she saw Violet's yellow paws. "Let's get you clean, shall we?" Alice sprinkled some baby oil onto a cloth and gently rubbed Violet's paws until every last bit of paint was gone.

"Don't see what you like about that cat," Uncle Leo mumbled. Alice was brushing Violet's fur from nose to tail, from ear to ear. "Seems like an awful lot of fuss to make over an animal."

"I don't know what I'd do without her," said Alice, peering into Violet's green eyes. "She always seems to know just when I need a good cuddle." And hearing that, Violet purred—just a little.

The next morning, Violet woke to the throaty call of the rooster and
a squeak of the screen door. *Who could be up so early?* She quietly slipped
from the foot of Alice's bed and was on the porch just as Uncle Leo
walked into the barn.

It must be milking time! Violet raced to catch up. The morning air was
cold, and though dawn was just beginning to soften the horizon, the light
inside the barn glowed with inviting warmth. Violet watched as Uncle
Leo sat on a stool next to a cow, but she decided to keep her distance.
The last thing Violet wanted to do was to get in Uncle Leo's way.

Uncle Leo's hands began to move in steady rhythm, and he talked in
a low, soothing voice to the cow. Two long streams of milk shot into the
pail between his feet.

In time, Uncle Leo stood up, moved the pail to the side, and stepped out of the stall. Quietly, carefully, Violet eased over to see how much milk he had collected. How warm and sweet it looked!

Just then, the cowed mooed, "Good morning!" and Violet jumped. But that startled the cow, who moved left, then right, then left again to avoid stepping on Violet. Her heart pounding with fear, Violet danced right, then left, then right again. Suddenly—*bang!* The cow kicked the pail, and over it went, spreading frothy white milk through the straw.

Oh no! thought Violet as she licked drops of creamy milk from her paws. But she didn't have long to savor the taste. . . .

"Lord, have mercy!" Uncle Leo said, throwing up his hands. Even the cow looked grumpy. "Cat, what in the dickens are you up to now? Go on, scoot!"

Violet didn't wait to hear any more. She dove behind the hay bale and hid there until Uncle Leo cleaned up and left.

Soon, Violet heard Uncle Leo grumbling that there wouldn't be any warm milk for his oatmeal this morning. "She didn't mean any harm," said Aunt Lydia. "It's in a cat's nature to go exploring, you know."

Violet slinked away to a quiet place under the old tractor. She couldn't bear the thought of getting in Uncle Leo's way again.

In the afternoon, Violet saw Aunt Lydia, Uncle Leo, and Alice make their way across the sheep paddock toward the orchards. There wouldn't be any paint cans or milk pails there, and she'd stay clear of everyone's feet.

Violet ducked under the gate and started up the hill. She stopped to chase a butterfly as it flew lazily through the tall grasses. When she looked up, she was startled to see a big white dog just a few feet away.

The dog noticed her and his ears perked up. Then his tail started wagging from side to side. *He wouldn't . . .* Violet thought, her green eyes going wide. *He doesn't mean to chase me, does he?*

But even as she watched, the dog started running straight for her!

Quick as a flash, Violet made for the big oak tree, scrambling higher and higher and higher until she felt safe enough to look back.

"What are you doing up there?" the dog asked from far below.

Violet tried her best to look relaxed, but her tail was as full as a topsail in high wind. "I thought you were chasing me!" she called to him.

"Naaahh . . ." said the dog. "Just having a little fun. Climb on down. I'm too old for chasing cats. Besides, I have work to do." And he wandered back to the sheep he was tending.

Violet's heart beat faster. *Climb down?* She had never climbed up a tree before, let alone down. Violet tested her footing, but the leaves rustled and the branch seemed sure to break. She couldn't do it. Climbing up had been instinct, but getting down? That was another matter.

It seemed like hours passed before Violet spotted Aunt Lydia, Uncle Leo, and Alice returning from the orchards. At last! Alice would come looking for her now.

But instead, the three of them crossed the far end of the paddock and went along to the farmhouse, their baskets piled high with apples. Violet meowed as loudly as she could, but she was too far from the house for anyone to hear.

As dusk came, the sky turned a soft purple. Even the sheep, who had grazed lazily all afternoon, began to gather in for the night. Violet watched as Alice stepped onto the porch and called to her.

"Here I am!" Violet meowed back, but Alice could not hear her. *What if no one finds me?* Violet thought with a heavy heart as she watched Alice go back inside. At that moment, Violet had never felt so little or so alone.

Just when Violet began to give up hope, Uncle Leo came out into the yard. He looked under the porch stairs. He looked in the barn. He looked in the henhouses. Then he turned and looked directly at the oak tree.

Uncle Leo? thought Violet. He couldn't be looking for her, could he? Not after all the trouble she had caused. But then Uncle Leo started walking toward the paddock. And he kept right on coming, through the gate and up the hill, until he was standing directly beneath the tree's graceful branches. Violet gave a tentative meow.

"Cat," said Uncle Leo, "what have you got up to now?" And with that, he turned and walked off to the barn. Violet's heart sank.

But then he reappeared in the barn door, a tall ladder tucked under his arm. Aunt Lydia and Alice—*Alice!*—came out of the house and followed him over to the tree.

"Oh! My poor Violet!" cried Alice. "I've been searching everywhere— I even looked in the pie cupboard. How did you know she'd be up there?"

"When we headed to the orchards, I saw that white tail waving through the grass as clear as a flag," Uncle Leo said. "I figured a cat as curious as this one would probably get herself up a tree one way or another."

A few minutes later, Uncle Leo had climbed to the highest rung of the ladder, but though he stretched and stretched, Violet was still too far for him to reach.

Uncle Leo sighed. "Now look here, cat," he said. "I can't come out to you, so you're going to have to come to me."

Violet trembled. Uncle Leo looked so far away, and the ground was so far below.

"Have faith, cat," said Uncle Leo quietly. "I won't let you fall." And he stretched his arms as far as they would reach.

Violet gave a small meow and put out one tentative paw. The branch seemed to waver, and the leaves rustled. But Uncle Leo held his arms steady. *He won't let me fall*, thought Violet. And with that, she took one, two, three little steps across the length of the branch and straight into Uncle Leo's arms. "There, now, cat," Uncle Leo said as he tucked Violet into his jacket to warm her up. Violet could feel his heart beating as fast as hers.

Uncle Leo carefully made his way down the ladder. Then he handed Violet to Alice, who cuddled and cooed to her until Violet felt quite safe again. "Sometimes it's hard to be a little cat in such a big world, isn't it?" said Alice as she gently kissed Violet's head. And hearing that, Violet had to purr—just a little.

Later that night, everyone gathered on the porch to enjoy a slice of warm apple pie and gaze up at the stars. As Violet watched, tiny lights began to sparkle across the grass. *Could they be stars, too?* She flicked her tail in curiosity, then quickly held herself still: curiosity had gotten her into enough trouble.

"The last fireflies of the season," said Aunt Lydia.

"They're like God's earth-bound stars," said Alice wistfully. "We don't see many fireflies in the city."

As Alice and Aunt Lydia chatted, Violet glanced at Uncle Leo. He looked so tired, and she wished she knew how to thank him for rescuing her. Then she had an idea.

Violet tiptoed over to him and nudged his leg ever so gently with her head. A good cuddle always made Alice feel better, but would Uncle Leo want anything to do with her after all the trouble she'd caused?

Uncle Leo looked down at her. "Never was much of a cat person," he announced. Then he leaned down and lowered his voice. "But I suppose I could make an exception for you."

As the last fireflies of the season glimmered in the cool night air, Uncle Leo scooped Violet onto his lap and gave her the softest of rubs behind her ear. And she began to purr—quite a lot.